ZEBRA'S HICCUPS

For Satoshi and Yoko

Copyright © 1991 by David McKee
This paperback edition first published in 2003. The rights of David McKee to be identified as the author
and illustrator of this work has been asserted by him in accordance with the Copyright, Designs and Patents Act, 1988.
First published in Great Britain in 1991 by Andersen Press Ltd. 20 Vauxhall Bridge Road, London SW1V 2SA.
Published in Australia by Random House Australia Pty., 20 Alfred Street, Milsons Point, Sydney, NSW 2061.
All rights reserved. Colour separated in Switzerland by Photolitho, Zürich.
Printed and bound in Italy by Grafiche AZ, Verona.

10 9 8 7 6 5 4 3 2

British Library Cataloguing in Publication Data available.

ISBN 1 84270 221 1

This book has been printed on acid-free paper

ZEBRA'S HICCUPS
DaVid McKee

Andersen Press · London

The animals loved to play.
"Come and play, Zebra," they called. "This is fun."
"No thank you, I am busy," Zebra answered. He was a
very serious and dignified zebra.

One day, Zebra got hiccups.
"Oh my, how extremely inconvenient HIC," he said to
himself. "I shall simply, HIC, ignore them and go out for
a walk. Perhaps they will disappear.

"Hi there, Zebra," said Tiger.

"Good HIC, ah. Good morning HIC," said Zebra.

"Hiccups!" said Tiger. "Don't worry I know a cure. Hold your breath, close your eyes, and say the alphabet backwards."

"That sounds much too HIC silly," said Zebra.

"Yoo hoo, Zebra," called Miss Pig. "Come skating with me."

"Good morning Miss P HIC," said Zebra.

"Hiccups?" asked Miss Pig. "I know a great cure. Put your head between your knees and drink a glass of water upside down."

"No HIC you," said Zebra. "That is far too un-HIC dignified for me."

"Zebra's got hiccups," said Little Elephant. "When I get hiccups I stand on one leg and go, 'too d'loo d'loo d'loo d'loo,' as long as I can."
"Me too," grinned Big Elephant.
"But definitely not me, HIC," said Zebra.
Next Zebra met Crocodile.

"Shoot baskets with me," said Crocodile.

"No, thank you Croco HIC," said Zebra.

"Oh-oh, who has hiccups?" said Crocodile. "Here's a sure fire hicketty cure. Stand on your head, hold the ball between your legs and sing. Clicketty, click. Works every time."

"I'm sure," said Zebra. "HIC."

Then, something strange began to happen. The hiccuping began to move Zebra's stripes. The more he hiccuped the more his stripes bumped together. Zebra never noticed.

It was Mrs Duck who told him.
"Is that you Zebra?" she said. "You do look strange."
"You mean HIC sound strange," said Zebra. "It's hiccups."
"I mean look strange. Look at yourself," said Mrs Duck.

"OH NO," groaned Zebra. "Just look what has happened.
I look HICdiculous. My wonderful stripes."

"I should have tried the cures," said Zebra. "What was it that Tiger said? I can't remember HIC."
He hurried back to find Tiger.

At Tiger's, Zebra took a deep breath, closed his eyes and said, "ZYXV no W HIC. Oh dear, HIC I mean ZYXWVUT HIC RS NO SR HIC."

Tiger chuckled and Zebra opened his eyes.
"This will never work," he sighed. "I'm off to try Miss
Pig's HIC. It's not funny you HIC know."
"I think it's very funny," said Tiger. "Wait for me."

Miss Pig gave Zebra a glass of water and said, "Head between your knees and drink this upside down." Zebra sat and drank and coughed and spluttered and choked and finally hiccuped.

"HIC. Absolutely HICely hopeless, and very HIC messy,"
said Zebra with a little smile. "Let's try Elephant's cure."

"I'll help you Zebra," said Little Elephant. "Stand on one leg and 'too d'loo d'loo d'loo' as long as you can." Zebra went "too d'loo d'HIC d'loo d'loo HIC loo d'loo HIC," until the others laughed.

Zebra grinned. "Totally useless. Come on HIC. Maybe HICodile's clicketty cure can stop these hicketty HICcups."

"First a headstand," said Crocodile. "Ball between your legs. Now sing."
Zebra just laughed and so did all the others.

"It doesn't work if you laugh," giggled Crocodile.
"I can't help HIC, it," said Zebra, and he fell over still laughing.

Mrs Duck came along to see what all the noise was about.
"He can't HIC for ever," she said.
Then, keeping her voice low so that Zebra wouldn't hear,
she told the others what to do.

Zebra was recovering from laughing when he was drenched by cold water.
"Now that's not funny," he said. "Not funny at all." But there was not one HIC.

"The shock has worked! He's cured," said Mrs Duck.
"Hooray," shouted all the animals.
"But I do feel strange without my stripes," said Zebra.

The cold water made him shiver. Then he sneezed a huge sneeze. The sneeze did the trick. It shook the stripes back into place. "Two cures in one," said Zebra. "Thank you all."

"You've caught a chill," said Tiger. "I know a great cure."
"So do I, so do I," the others all shouted together.
"And so do I," laughed Zebra as he waved goodbye to
his friends.
"I wonder what we'll play tomorrow?" he thought as
he hurried home to a hot bath, a hot drink and a nice
warm bed . . .

More Andersen Press paperback picture books!

Ruggles
by Anne Fine and Ruth Brown

Betty's Not Well Today
by Gus Clarke

War and Peas
by Michael Foreman

The Sad Story of Veronica Who Played the Violin
by David McKee

The Wrong Overcoat
by Hiawyn Oram and Mark Birchall

Lazy Jack
by Tony Ross

Rabbit's Wish
by Paul Stewart and Chris Riddell

Mr Bear and the Bear
by Frances Thomas and Ruth Brown

What Did I Look Like When I Was a Baby?
by Jeanne Willis and Tony Ross